This edition published by Parragon in 2009
Parragon
Queen Street House
4 Queen Street
Bath BA1 1HE, UK

ISBN 978-1-4075-8191-0

Printed in China

Cinderella

My Perfect Wedding

By Lisa Ann Marsoli • Illustrated by the Disney Storybook Artists

Bath · New York · Singapore · Hong Kong · Cologne · Delhi · Melbourne

*C*inderella's dreams were coming true at last! She and the Prince were going to be married, and a new life filled with happiness would soon begin.

But first, there was a wedding to plan. . . .

Prudence, Cinderella's lady-in-waiting, was in charge of the planning. She had a very long list of tasks.

"Excuse me," Cinderella asked Prudence, "couldn't we just have a simple wedding?"

Prudence frowned. "Cinderella, now that you are going to be a princess, you must start thinking big!"

Later, Prudence arrived with the royal dressmaker and several wedding gowns.

"Do you think you can design something . . . plainer?" Cinderella asked politely.

"Certainly not!" Prudence said. "Plain and princess do not go together!"

Next it was time to select the flowers. The florist greeted them with . . . a rosebush!

"Do you have something a bit . . . smaller?" Cinderella asked.

"This is perfect," Prudence said. "You just have to know how to carry it." Prudence held the flowers out in front of her and – buzzzz – she was stung by a bee!

"Prudence has gone to bed to nurse her bee sting. I'll have to plan the wedding myself," Cinderella said to the mice. "Now, what should I do first?"

"Who's-a comin', Cinderelly?" asked Jaq.

"The guest list! Good idea, Jaq. Well, of course all of you are invited," Cinderella replied. "And my Fairy Godmother . . . I wish she were here right now."

Suddenly, a twinkling light filled the room, and Cinderella's Fairy Godmother appeared! "We'll plan an absolutely magical wedding for you, my dear," she said, giving Cinderella a big hug. "Now, when is it exactly?"

Gus counted on his fingers. "Tomorrow!" he announced.

"Oh, my goodness, child!" cried the Fairy Godmother.

"Lots ta do!" Jaq added.

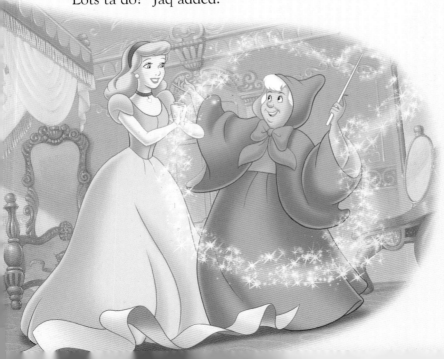

"Well, then, let's start at the beginning – with the dress!" the Fairy Godmother said. She waved her wand, and Cinderella found herself in an elegant white gown. But her Fairy Godmother had forgotten the veil.

"It's lovely," Cinderella said, "but don't you think it needs . . . ?"

The Fairy Godmother wasn't listening. She was already working on the next task – invitations! In moments, hundreds of lovely pink cards sat in stacks around the room.

"Now we shall prepare the feast and make the cake!" she announced.

Cinderella changed out of her gown and followed her Fairy Godmother to the royal kitchen. The mice picked up where the Fairy Godmother had left off. Mary, Suzy and Perla pulled out a box of tiny pearls and began making a veil.

And Jaq gave each of the other mice an armload of invitations to deliver. Unfortunately, they didn't get very far before Pom-Pom the cat showed up!

"Whew! Close-a call!" said Jaq as he and Gus raced away from Pom-Pom and scurried into the kitchen. They arrived just in time to help the Fairy Godmother create a great big, fancy cake!

Cinderella tried to hide her disappointment. "Um . . . Prudence will love it," she said. "You know, I really should see how she's feeling."

"Poor child," the Fairy Godmother said after Cinderella had left. "These wedding plans must be too much for her."

Jaq and Gus tugged at the Fairy Godmother's sleeve.

"Cinderelly likes smaller things," Jaq told her. "Like mice!"

All at once, the Fairy Godmother understood.

Later, the Fairy Godmother took Cinderella's hand.
"I'm afraid I may have gotten a bit carried away, my dear,"
the Fairy Godmother confessed. "Now, tell me, child, what
would the wedding of your dreams be like?"

After listening to Cinderella, the Fairy Godmother finished the beautiful veil. Then she got rid of all the invitations by magically sending them to destinations near and far.

"Now let's cut that cake down to size," the Fairy Godmother said.

As they left for the kitchen, Cinderella turned toward the kindhearted mice. "Thank you, my little friends," she said gratefully.

The next day, Cinderella looked lovely in her simple white gown, veil and gloves. But something was missing.

"Good heavens, child!" the Fairy Godmother exclaimed. "You can't get married in your bare feet!" She waved her wand, and Cinderella's beautiful glass slippers peeked out from underneath her gown.

After the ceremony, the Prince and Cinderella shared a joyous celebration with their guests. Even Prudence was pleased.

"However did you manage all of this?" the Prince asked his new princess.

Cinderella smiled and said, "With friends by your side, anything is possible!"

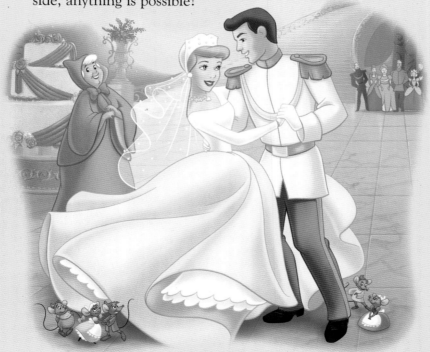